Katie Woo

Katie's Noisy Music

by Fran Manushkin

illustrated by Tammie Lyon

PICTURE WINDOW BOOKS
a capstone imprint

Katie Woo is published by Picture Window Books,
A Capstone Imprint
1710 Roe Crest Drive
North Mankato, Minnesota 56003
www.capstonepub.com

Text © 2015 Fran Manushkin
Illustrations © 2015 Picture Window Books

Library of Congress Cataloging-in-Publication Data
Manushkin, Fran, author.
  Katie's noisy music / by Fran Manushkin; illustrated by Tammie Lyon.
      pages cm. — (Katie Woo)
  Summary: Katie Woo wants to learn an instrument, but she is having trouble deciding what kind of music suits her best.
    ISBN 978-1-4795-5893-3 (hardcover)
    ISBN 978-1-4795-5895-7 (paperback)
    ISBN 978-1-4795-6195-7 (eBook)
1. Woo, Katie (Fictitious character)—Juvenile fiction. 2. Chinese Americans—Juvenile fiction. 3. Musical instruments—Juvenile fiction. 4. Choice (Psychology)—Juvenile fiction. [1. Musical instruments—Fiction. 2. Music—Fiction. 3. Choice—Fiction. 4. Chinese Americans—Fiction.] I. Lyon, Tammie, illustrator. II. Title. III. Series: Manushkin, Fran. Katie Woo.

  PZ7.M3195Kcr 2015
  813.54—dc23   2014022382

Art Director: Heather Kindseth Wutschke
Graphic Designer: Kristi Carlson

Photo Credits:
Greg Holch, pg. 26
Tammie Lyon, pg. 26

Printed in the United States of America in Stevens Point, Wisconsin.
        092014   008479WZS15

Table of Contents

Chapter 1

Music of Her Own

Katie's father was playing

the piano. Katie loved the

sounds he made.

She told her dad, "Your

music makes me happy."

"You can make music too," said Katie's dad. "I can teach you to play the piano."

Katie played a few notes. They made a nice plinking sound.

"Hmm," said Katie, "I like the piano. But I'd like to play something of my own."

"I'll ask JoJo what to play," said Katie.

As she walked to JoJo's house, Katie ran a stick along a fence. She liked the *clickity-clackity* sound.

Katie asked JoJo, "What do you like to play?"

"I love my guitar," said JoJo. She played "This Land Is Your Land," and Katie sang along.

"I can teach you to play

the guitar," offered JoJo.

"That would be fun," said

Katie. "But I'd like to play

something of my own."

Chapter 2

More Music Makers!

The next night, Katie and her parents went to a school concert.

"I'd like to be on that stage," said Katie. "I love the sound of clapping!"

After the concert, Pedro
let Katie try his violin.

"Yikes!" she yelled. "My
ears hurt."

"It takes a while to learn
it," said Pedro.

"No, thanks!" said Katie.

Mattie let Katie try

playing her cello. It

squawked and squealed.

"No way am I playing

this," sighed Katie. "Isn't

there anything I can play?"

Katie was so unhappy,

she kicked a can all the way

home. It made a fine *clinking*

and *clanking* sound.

Katie went to bed that night feeling sad. But when it began raining, the *pitter-patter* of the raindrops made her feel cozy. She fell asleep with a smile.

On Saturday, Barry took Katie to his accordion lesson at the music store.

"Let me try!" said Katie. "Wowza! It's nice and noisy but kind of heavy. Bye-bye, accordion!"

While she waited for Barry,

Katie tried playing a flute.

"It's very skinny," she said.

So she tried the tuba.

"It's too big!" sighed Katie.

"Nothing is right for me."

Chapter 3

Click-Clack-Click

At dinner that night, Katie was so unhappy, she wasn't hungry. She just clicked her chopsticks together. *Click-clack-click.*

"Do that again," said Katie's mom.

Katie did: *click-clack click.*

"I like that sound," said

her mom.

Katie clicked some more.

"Guess what?" said her

dad. "You are making music."

Katie banged a spoon on

a pot. "Is this music too?"

she asked.

"Yes!" Her dad smiled.

"Yay!" said Katie,

jumping up and down. "I

know what I want to play!"

"THE DRUMS!" they all said together.

"Absolutely!" added Katie's dad. "Katie and the drums were made for each other."

Katie began learning to play the drums. She made them go *click-clack, clank-clank,* and *boom-boom-BOOM!*

She made soft *tip-tip-tapping* sounds and *pitter-patter* raindrop sounds. All the sounds were music.

At the next school concert, Katie played the drums. As she took a bow, she said, "Music makes me happy!"

It made everyone else happy, too.

About the Author

Fran Manushkin is the author of many
popular picture books, including *Baby,
Come Out!*; *Latkes and Applesauce: A
Hanukkah Story*; *The Tushy Book*; *The Belly Book*;
and *Big Girl Panties*. There is a real Katie Woo — she's Fran's
great-niece — but she never gets in half the trouble of the
Katie Woo in the books. Fran writes on her beloved Mac
computer in New York City, without the help of her
two naughty cats, Chaim and Goldy.

About the Illustrator

Tammie Lyon began her love for drawing
at a young age while sitting at the kitchen
table with her dad. She continued her love
of art and eventually attended the Columbus College of
Art and Design, where she earned a bachelor's degree in fine
art. After a brief career as a professional ballet dancer, she
decided to devote herself full time to illustration. Today she
lives with her husband, Lee, in Cincinnati, Ohio. Her dogs, Gus
and Dudley, keep her company as she works in her studio.

Glossary

accordion (uh-KOR-dee-uhn)—a musical instrument that you squeeze to make sound and play by pressing keys and buttons

cello (CHEL-oh)—a large stringed instrument that rests on the floor. It is played with a bow like a violin but is held between the knees.

clanking (KLANG-keeng)—a sharp sound often produced by metal hitting something

clinking (KLING-keeng)—a light, sharp, ringing sound

piano (pee-AN-oh)—a large keyboard instrument that produces musical sounds when padded hammers inside the piano strike tuned metal strings

plinking (PLING-keeng)—a short, light, ringing sound

violin (vye-uh-LIN)—a musical instrument with four strings, played with a bow

Discussion Questions

1. The author uses onomatopoeia, or sound words, in the story. Why do you think she chose to do so? Can you think of other sound words?

2. Katie says she wants to play an instrument of her own. What does that mean? Why do you think she felt that way?

3. Music makes many of the characters in the story feel happy. How does music make you feel?

Writing Prompts

1. Imagine Katie has a new album coming out. Create an album cover for her. Be sure to name the album and several songs.

2. List the sound words used in the story. Then write a poem that uses at least three of the words.

3. Choose your favorite instrument in the story. Then write a persuasive paper to convince a reader that it is the best instrument to play.

Having Fun with Katie Woo!

Drums and other percussion instruments are used all over the world. You can make your own Chinese drum, perfect for playing at Chinese New Year or anytime!

Chinese Drum

What you need:

- 2 small paper plates
- popsicle stick
- hot glue gun and glue
- hole punch
- two 7-inch ribbons
- 2 beads

What you do:

1. Using the hot glue gun, glue the popsicle stick to the top of one of the paper plate edges to make the drum's handle.

2. Hot glue the two paper plates together.

3. Use the hole punch to punch a hole on each side of the drum.

4. String a ribbon through each hole and tie a knot to secure it. Then tie a bead on the other end of each ribbon.

Your drum is ready to play! Twist the handle back and forth to make the beads tap on the plates. You can also decorate your drum with drawings, Chinese characters, or pieces of colorful paper. Be creative and have fun!

THE FUN DOESN'T STOP HERE!

Discover more at www.capstonekids.com

- Videos & Contests
- Games & Puzzles
- Friends & Favorites
- Authors & Illustrators

Find cool websites and more books like this one at www.facthound.com. Just type in the Book ID: **9781479558933** and you're ready to go!